WE'RE ALL WONDERS

WRITTEN AND ILLUSTRATED BY R. J. PALACIO

Alfred A. Knopf • New York

For Nathaniel Newman, a true wonder,
and his wonder of a family, Magda, Russel, and Jake.

For Dina Zuckerberg and the MyFace family.
You are my heroes.

THIS IS A BORZOI BOOK PUBLISHED BY ALFRED A. KNOPF

Copyright © 2017 by R. J. Palacio

All rights reserved. Published in the United States by Alfred A. Knopf, an imprint of
Random House Children's Books, a division of Penguin Random House LLC, New York.
Originally published in the United States as a jacketed hardcover by
Alfred A. Knopf, an imprint of Random House Children's Books, a division of
Penguin Random House LLC, New York, in 2017.

Knopf, Borzoi Books, and the colophon are registered trademarks of
Penguin Random House LLC. Read Together, Be Together and the colophon are
trademarks of Penguin Random House LLC.

"8 Ways to Make the Most of Storytime" copyright © 2020 by Meredith Corporation. All rights
reserved. Reprinted with permission.

Visit us on the Web! rhcbooks.com

Educators and librarians, for a variety of teaching tools, visit us at RHTeachersLibrarians.com

Library of Congress Cataloging-in-Publication Data is available upon request.
ISBN 978-1-5247-6649-8 (trade) — ISBN 978-1-5247-6650-4 (lib. bdg.) —
ISBN 978-1-5247-6651-1 (ebook) —
ISBN 978-0-593-30340-5 (Read Together, Be Together)

A note on the art in this book: I based Auggie's look in this picture book on the iconic jacket for
Wonder, which was art-directed by Isabel Warren-Lynch and beautifully envisioned and drawn
by the artistic wonder Tad Carpenter. I am ever thankful for their collaboration, which resulted
in an image that has captured the imagination of readers everywhere. I drew all the line art for
these illustrations with an iPencil in Procreate for the iPad, and used a combination of painting
(with the stylus) and Photoshop to create the final art.

MANUFACTURED IN CHINA
10 9 8 7 6 5 4 3 2 1

2020 Read Together, Be Together Edition

8 Ways to Make the Most of Storytime

FROM THE EDITORS OF

Parents.

① BE AS DRAMATIC AS POSSIBLE.

It'll help the story stick in your child's memory. You could give the mouse a British accent, make the lion roar, or speak very slowly when you're reading the snail's dialogue. Have fun making sound effects for words like boom, moo, or achoo. Encourage your child to act out movements, slithering like a snake or leaping like a frog.

② INVITE SPECIAL GUESTS.

Ask your kids if their favorite stuffed animal, action figure, or doll would like to listen too. Or curl up with the family pet. Including the whole gang will help hold their interest and make storytime seem more special. But if your child does start to lose interest before you've reached the last page, that's okay because half a book here or a quarter of a book there still counts as reading!

③ KEEP LOVINGLY WORN BOOKS IN THE ROTATION.

There's a reason your kids ask for the same title again and again: A familiar story can be as comforting as a favorite blankie. The characters become their friends, and the books serve an important emotional purpose.

④ PLAY A GUESSING GAME.

When reading a new book, pause a few times to challenge your kids to predict what's going to happen next. Encourage them to refer to the title and illustrations for clues.

⑤ REFLECT ON THE STORY.

Talk about a book for a few minutes before you move on to another. Start a conversation with statements like "I'm wondering...," "I wish I could ask the author...," and "I'm getting the idea..." This helps develop your children's intuition and their ability to communicate a story back to you.

READ TOGETHER, BE TOGETHER
is a nationwide movement developed by Penguin Random House in partnership with *Parents* magazine that celebrates the importance, and power, of the shared reading experience between an adult and a child. Reading aloud regularly to babies and young children is one of the most effective ways to foster early literacy and is a key factor responsible for building language and social skills. READ TOGETHER, BE TOGETHER offers parents the tips and tools to make family reading a regular and cherished activity.

⑥ CONNECT STORIES WITH WHAT'S HAPPENING IN REAL LIFE.

Suppose you read your child a story about a baby bird, and a day or two later, you spot a tiny sparrow in the park. Ask your child, "Doesn't that bird look like the one in the book we read yesterday? I wonder if it's looking for its mommy too?" Doing so will help promote information recall and build vocabulary.

⑦ CREATE AN IMPROVISED READING NOOK.

Storytime on the sofa or a cozy chair is sweet, but wouldn't your kids lose their mind if you set up a fort every now and then? It doesn't have to be fancy: Just drape a blanket over two chairs, grab a couple of pillows, and squeeze in.

⑧ ALWAYS BE THE STORYTELLER AT BEDTIME.

You'll feel so proud when your little ones start recognizing and sounding out words on their own. But resist asking them to read to you at bedtime because it would replace this warm, wonderful bonding ritual with something that can feel like work for kids. Plus, they'll be able to listen to a more complicated book than they can read on their own.

I know I'm not an ordinary kid.

Sure, I do ordinary things.

I ride a bike.

I eat ice cream.

I play ball.

I just don't look ordinary.

I don't look like other kids.

My mom says I'm unique.
She says I'm a wonder.

My dog, Daisy, agrees!

But some people don't see
that I'm a wonder.

All they see
is how different I look.

Sometimes they
stare at me.

They point or laugh.

They even say
mean things
behind my back.

But I can hear them.

It hurts my feelings.

It hurts Daisy's feelings, too.

When that happens, I put on my helmet.

I put Daisy's helmet on, too. And then we...

BLAST OFF!

Up! Up! Up!
Up through the clouds...

across the galaxy...

...all the way to Pluto!

We say hello to old friends.

From far away, the Earth looks so small. I can't see any people. But I know they're there.

Billions of people. People of all different colors. People who walk and talk differently. People who look different. Like me!

The Earth is big enough for all kinds of people.

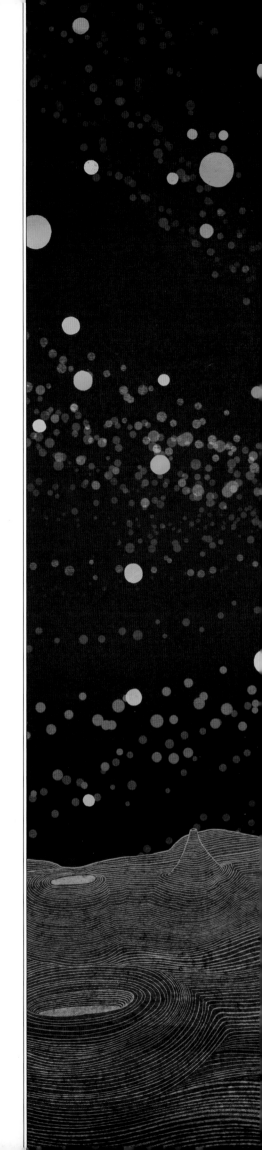

I know I can't change the way I look.

But maybe, just maybe…

...people can change the way they see.

If they do, they'll see that I'm a wonder.

And they'll see that they're wonders, too.

We're all wonders!

Look with kindness and you will always find wonder.